LENTIL

LENTIL

BY ROBERT McCLOSKEY

The Viking Press · New York

VIKING KESTREL
Viking Penguin Inc., 40 West 23rd Street, New York, New York 10010, U.S.A.
Penguin Books Ltd, 27 Wrights Lane, London W8 5TZ (Publishing & Editorial), and
Harmondsworth, Middlesex, England (Distribution & Warehouse)
Penguin Books Australia Ltd, Ringwood, Victoria, Australia
Penguin Books Canada Limited, 2801 John Street, Markham, Ontario, Canada L3R 1B4
Penguin Books (N.Z.) Ltd, 182–190 Wairau Road, Auckland 10, New Zealand

Copyright © Robert McCloskey, 1940
Copyright renewed © Robert McCloskey, 1968
All rights reserved
First published in 1940 by The Viking Press
Published simultaneously in Canada
Printed in the United States of America

23 25 27 29 30 28 26 24 22

Library of Congress catalog number: 40-8617
ISBN 0-670-42357-2

LENTIL

*ALSO
WRITTEN AND ILLUSTRATED
BY ROBERT McCLOSKEY*

In the town of Alto, Ohio, there lived a boy named Lentil.

Lentil had a happy life except for one thing—he wanted to sing, but he couldn't!

It was most embarrassing, because when he opened his mouth to try, only strange sounds came out....

And he couldn't even whistle because he couldn't pucker his lips.

But he did want to make music, so he saved up enough pennies to buy a harmonica.

Lentil was proud of his new harmonica and he decided to become an expert. So he played a lot, whenever and wherever he could.

His favorite place to practice was in the bathtub, because there the tone was improved one hundred per cent.

He used to play almost all the way to school. Down Vine Street to the corner of Main, past the finest house in Alto, which belonged to the great Colonel Carter. Then . . .

past the drug store,
the barber shop, and the
Alto Library, which was a gift of
the great Colonel Carter,

by the Methodist Church, through the Carter Memorial Park, and around the Soldiers and Sailors Monument that the Colonel had built there.

Then Lentil would stuff his harmonica into his pocket and take a short cut up the alley behind the hardware store so he would not be late for school.

People would smile and wave hello to Lentil as he walked down the street, because everyone in Alto liked Lentil's music; that is, everybody but Old Sneep. Old Sneep didn't like much of anything or anybody. He just sat on a park bench and whittled and grumbled.

One day the news got around that the great Colonel Carter, who had been away for two years, was coming home. People began to plan a grand welcome, but when Old Sneep heard the news he said: "Humph! We wuz boys together. He ain't a mite better'n you or me and he needs takin' down a peg or two." Sneep just kept right on whittling, but everybody else kept right on planning. Colonel Carter was the town's most important citizen, so . . .

the people hung out flags and decorated the streets. The mayor
prepared a speech, the Alto Brass Band put on their new uni-
forms, and the printer, the grocer, the plumber, the minister, the
barber, the druggist, the ice man, the school teachers, the house-
wives and their husbands and their children—yes,

the whole town went to the station to welcome Colonel Carter.

The train pulled in. The musicians in the band were waiting for the leader to signal them to play, the leader was waiting for the mayor to nod to him to start the band, and the mayor was waiting for Colonel Carter to step from his private car. All the people held their breath and waited.

Then there was a wet sound from above.

There sat Old Sneep, sucking on a lemon.

Old Sneep knew that when the musicians looked at him their mouths would pucker up so they could not play their horns. The whole band looked up at Old Sneep. The mayor gave the signal to play, but the cornetist couldn't play his cornet, the piccolo player couldn't

play his piccolo, the trombone player couldn't play his trombone, and the tuba player couldn't play his tuba, because their lips were all puckered up.

They couldn't play a single note! The musicians just stood there holding their instruments and looking up at Sneep sucking on the lemon. The leader looked helpless, the people were too surprised to move or say a thing, and the mayor wrung his hands and wore a look that said: "Can't somebody do something, please!"

As Colonel Carter stepped from his car, the only sound was the noise of Sneep's lemon.

Clouds began to gather on the colonel's brow and he said: "Hmph" in an indignant sort of way.

Of course Lentil's lips were not puckered and he knew that something had to be done. So he took out his harmonica and started to play "Comin' 'round the Mountain When She Comes."

When Lentil began to play the second chorus, Colonel Carter smiled.

Then he let out a loud chuckle and began to sing "Driving Six White Horses When She Comes."

Then everybody sang and they all marched down Main Street behind the colonel's car.

Lentil rode with the colonel, who took a turn at the harmonica when Lentil's wind began to give out. (He said that he hadn't played one since he was a boy, but he did very well considering.)

They marched to the colonel's house and paraded through the gate and onto the front lawn. The mayor's committee served ice cream cones to all the citizens and Colonel Carter made a speech saying how happy he was about such a fine welcome and how happy he was to be home again. When he said that he was going to build a new hospital for the town of Alto, everybody was happy — even Old Sneep!

So you never can tell what will happen when you learn to play the harmonica.